Frank Rodgers

MAC

and the Big Feet

MACDONALD YOUNG BOOKS

Dear Mac,
Please come on holiday with us on our first visit to the city.

We will stay at the Grand Hotel on Main Street.

Let's all have a wonderful time together!

With love from all your country cousins.

Mac was so excited he packed a bag
and left right away.
This was going to be his first visit
to the city too.

But the city was so big and so busy that Mac soon got lost.
"Excuse me," he called, "can anyone tell me where the
Grand Hotel on Main Street is, please?"

Nobody heard him.
"Excuse me," he called again,
then he had to jump like a kangaroo as
a huge foot nearly trod on him. "Watch out!" he squeaked.
Suddenly he saw the sign.
GRAND HOTEL
Mouse Entrance

Mac dashed through the crowd towards it.
"Excuse me! Watch out!" he cried,
but still nobody heard him.

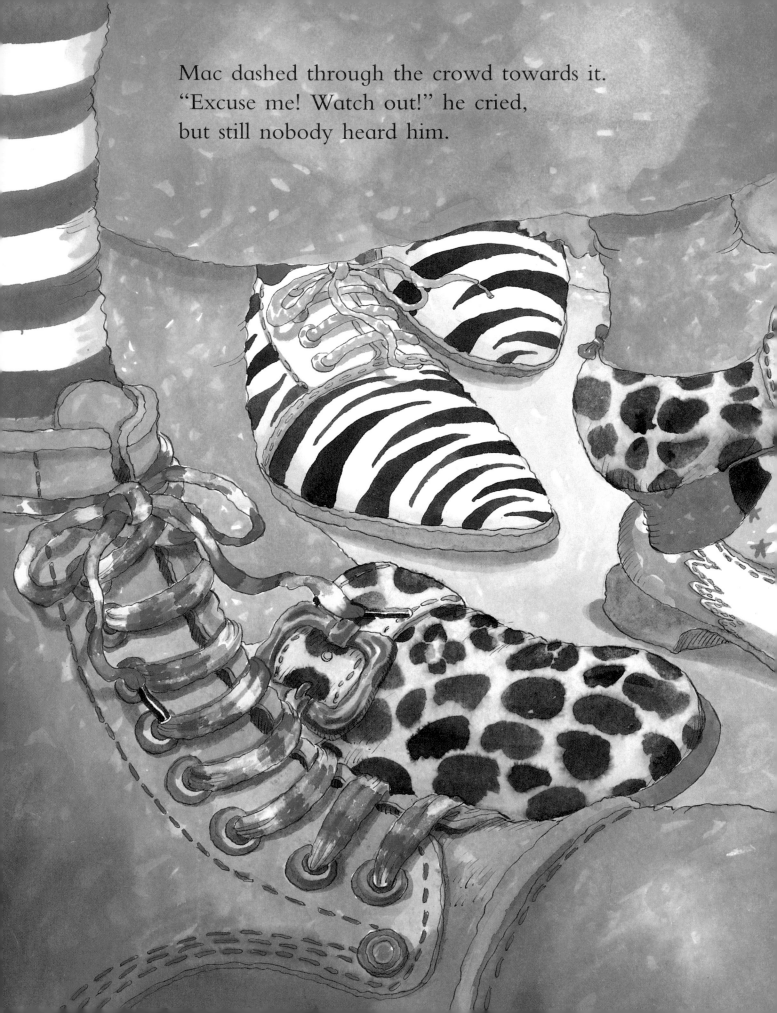

He dodged and darted and ducked beneath all the big feet. At last he reached the Mouse Entrance of the Grand Hotel and ran inside.

All his country cousins had just arrived too
and were delighted to see him.
"I'm glad you got here safely," said cousin Lucy
giving him a big hug.

"Yes, but I nearly got trodden on," said Mac.
"I know. It's terrible, isn't it?" said cousin Jack.
"I didn't know the city was so busy. I miss
the quiet of the country already!"

"So do we," said some of the country cousins.
"Maybe we should just go home again."
"But we haven't had our holiday yet," said Mac.
"I'm sure we'll have lots of fun here."

"Of course we will! We can swim in
the hotel's big pool," said cousin Mabel.

"We can dance in the hotel's big ballroom!"
said cousin Pattie.

"And we can go sightseeing in the city,"
said cousin Bobby.

"Wonderful!" laughed Mac. "What shall we do first?"
"Sightseeing!" cried the mice.

The city was full of wonderful sights,
but the mice didn't see any of them.

There were always big animals in the way.

They couldn't even sit down
to have a rest.

"Sightseeing?" snorted cousin Mabel. "Huh!
All we've seen in the city are big feet and big bottoms!"

"Why don't we go back to the hotel and have
a nice swim?" suggested Mac, and everyone agreed.

But the pool was packed.
Big feet sloshed and slapped all around Mac
and the country cousins. The mice wanted
to swim but they couldn't get near the water.

"Excuse me!" yelled Mac but nobody heard him
in the echoing noise. "Let's get out of here before
we get squashed," he said to everyone.
"Yes. Let's go dancing instead," said cousin Pattie.

The ballroom was bouncing fit to burst. Everyone was having a lovely time dancing and prancing, twirling and swirling. The mice tried to join in.

Bash! Crash! Big feet in twinkly high heels and
shiny shoes hit the floor, nearly stepping on
the country cousins once more.
"Excuse me!" cried Mac, but no one heard.

Clump! A big boot nearly stepped on Mac.

Thump! Cousin Tommy got kicked on the bottom.

Bump! A big foot trod on cousin Lucy's tail.

Whump! A high heel
just missed cousin Jack.

"Help! We've had enough!" cried the mice.
"This is a terrible holiday. We're going home!"
The country cousins ran for their lives.

Mac was left on his own.
"This isn't fair," he thought.
He shouted as loud as he could.
"EXCUSE ME!"
But nobody heard him
over the noise of the singer
and the band.

"What can I do?" thought Mac.
Then suddenly he had a brilliant idea.
Bravely he ran right into the middle of the ballroom.
He dodged and dived and ducked under all the big feet.

He reached the
bandstand and
climbed up like
a mountaineer.

Then he shinned up the
shiny microphone
stand as quickly
as a monkey.

When he got to the top he jumped on to
the singing rhino's nose and yelled into the microphone.

The music stopped.
The singing stopped.
The dancing stopped.
And the big feet stopped at last.

SE ME!!

"What's wrong?" asked everyone.
"I'm sorry I had to shout," said Mac,
"but nobody would listen. You are all so busy having
a good time that you've forgotten about the mice.
You nearly stepped on us."

"Oh, dear," everyone said, "we're very sorry.
We didn't realize we were being so thoughtless.
We were small ourselves once but we've
forgotten what it's like."

After that the big animals remembered about the mice.
They put up big signs all over the hotel...

Watch
your
step

Look
before you
leap

Mind
those
big feet

"It would be a good idea if you put up
signs all over the city too," said Mac,
and everyone agreed.

The country cousins were very proud of Mac.
And the hotel staff were so pleased that
everyone was having such a lovely time
that they made him a special cake.

When Mac saw it he laughed and laughed...
because the cake was shaped exactly like a pair of...

BIG FEET!